MARTIAN MASK

ISBN 0-590-50204-2

Published by Scholastic Inc.

12 11 10 9 8 7 6 5 4 3 2 1 6 7 8 9/9 0/0

Printed in the U.S.A. 23

First Scholastic printing, October 1996

Designed by Alfred Giuliani

Adapted by Laura O'Neill
Based on the television script by Steve Roberts
Illustrated by Aristides Ruiz

SCHOLASTIC INC.
New York Toronto London Auckland Sydney

Poor Stanley Ipkiss. He's very nice, but very shy. He has a boring job and a tiny apartment. His best friend is his little dog, Milo.

But Stanley has a secret. He is the owner of a very strange green mask. How strange? So strange that when Stanley puts it on, an awesome change comes over him. He becomes The Mask—a wild, zany, ever-changing, super-powered, show-off hero.

Stanley is always a little nervous about putting on the mask. He's so out of control when he's wearing it. He's never quite sure what he'll do. But, somehow, he can't resist it. When he's The Mask, he's cool. He's hot. He's . . . s-s-smokin'!

One night The Mask was happily zooming around Edge City in his Maskmobile. He whizzed past his old enemy, Lieutenant Kellaway, who was sitting in his police squad car with his assistant, Officer Doyle.

"Let's get him!" Kellaway growled as he stepped down hard on the gas pedal. "This time he won't get away!"

The Mask made Kellaway completely

crazy. Even though Kellaway suspected that The Mask was really Stanley, he could never prove it. Kellaway had vowed to stop The Mask's wild antics. But he'd have to catch him first.

"You are in violation of the law!" Kellaway shouted into a megaphone as he raced after the Maskmobile. "Pull your vehicle over now!" he roared, bumping into the Maskmobile from behind.

The Mask had to act fast. He pressed a switch and the Maskmobile began to twist and stretch. In seconds it turned into a Spacemaskmobile. The Mask was now dressed in a silver space suit. "Prepare for warp drive!" The Mask shouted. He hit a switch and the Spacemaskmobile zoomed away.

"I'm on ya, clown!" Kellaway cried, chasing after the Spacemaskmobile.

The Mask nosed the Spacemaskmobile into the sky. "Zow-ow-ow-ow!" he squealed. The Spacemaskmobile rocketed into outer space.

Kellaway jammed on his brakes. He leaped from the car and shook his fist at the sky. Once again, The Mask had escaped him. "He's got to come down sometime," Kellaway told Doyle.

Meanwhile, at a U.S. military outpost in the Antarctic, a strange blipping light appeared on the radar screen. "Sir, we've picked up the signal of an unidentified flying object," Agent Crosby alerted his boss. Crosby took a close-up photo of the object. Agent X studied the photograph carefully. He had no idea that he was looking at The Mask!

"The object has green skin," Agent X noted. "It must be an extraterrestrial. This could be a matter of cosmic importance, not to mention national security," he said. "Crosby, don't let that thing out of your sight!"

Suddenly, the blip on the screen took a sharp dive downward!

The Spacemaskmobile was crashing! "Ejector seat, engage!" The Mask cried, hoping to escape the ship before it crashed. But he was too late! The Spacemaskmobile smashed into an empty lot, sending up a huge cloud of smoke.

Was this the end of The Mask?

No way!

The ejector seat flung him into the air and slapped him against his apartment building. The Mask was flat as a pancake, but still smiling. "Home sweet home," he said with a sigh, as he slid down the side of the building.

Once inside his apartment, The Mask removed his mask and turned back into Stanley. He hid the mask and sat down

on his couch to rest. Milo sat at his side. Then Stanley turned on the TV. And who did he see? The Mask! "The Mask had another run-in with the authorities last night," the reporter said.

"I'm worried, Milo. They could be onto us," Stanley said. Milo looked up at Stanley and clicked the TV remote, changing the channel.

Stanley tried to forget about being The Mask. He turned his attention to a science-fiction movie about a creepy space alien. What Stanley didn't know was that he and Milo weren't the only ones paying attention to the movie. In an apartment building right across the way, others were listening in.

Agent X and Crosby had tracked the Spacemaskmobile right to Stanley's apartment. Now they were listening in on everything that was being said in Stanley's room. But what they were hearing was really the TV program. "Phase one of my mission is complete. I have assumed humanoid form," they heard the TV alien say. "I will now destroy the Earth creatures and pave the way for a total conquest of the planet."

That was all Agent X needed to hear. Now he was sure Stanley was an alien who had come to destroy the Earth. He whipped off his headphones and called his agents. "Red alert! We're going in to get that alien!"

Agent X, Crosby, and the other agents ran up the stairs to Stanley's apartment. On his way up, Agent X smacked right into . . .

Detective Kellaway! "Oof! Ah! Whoa!" both men sputtered as they tumbled to the floor.

"What are you? Some kind of nut?" Kellaway growled, sitting up.

Agent X flashed his badge. "Federal agent. This is a raid!"

Kellaway showed his badge. "Edge City Police Department! This is a stake-out!"

The two men began fighting about who was in charge. "Behind that door is an alien bent on taking over the world!" Agent X yelled.

"Alien?" Kellaway shouted in disbelief. "He's a common *criminal*!"

"You're interfering with a government operation, brickhead!" Agent X screamed. "Back off!"

Meanwhile, Stanley continued watching the outer-space movie in his apartment. He paid no attention to the noise in his hallway. Suddenly, the movie was interrupted by a special news flash. "A mutant with puttylike superpowers escaped from prison last night," the reporter stated. "He's with a big fish," she added with a laugh. A photo of the large fish appeared on the screen.

Stanley leaped from his chair. "That's no ordinary big fish! That's *Fish Guy*! And . . . and Putty-Thing. They're the Terrible Two! I've got to do something!" Putty-Thing and Fish Guy were no strangers to The Mask. He had tangled with the two super-villains before. Milo let out a long yowl and Stanley sat back down.

"In other news," the reporter continued, "the police are still looking for The Mask."

That report made Stanley sit up straight. If he caught Putty-Thing and Fish Guy, maybe Kellaway would leave him alone. Yes! He decided to do it. He put on the mask. With a big *woosh!* and a flash of light, he became Football Player Mask. "Let's do it team! Woof! Woof! Woof!" he cheered as the mask took on the shape of a football helmet.

"Break!" shouted Football Player Mask. Then he zoomed out the open window just as the apartment door behind him burst open. Kellaway, Doyle, Agent X, Crosby, and the other agents tumbled into the room.

"Freeze!" Kellaway commanded.

Milo gazed up at him.

"He's gone!" Agent X shouted. "This is all *your* fault!" he said to Kellaway.

Out in the desert, Putty-Thing and Fish Guy had stopped at a store for food. “Dude, how we gonna *pay* for this?” Putty-Thing asked Fish Guy, pointing to the bags of junk food on the counter. Fish Guy was more worried about how he smelled. Ever since an accident had turned him into a fish, he stank! “Do I reek?” Fish Guy asked Putty-Thing.

Putty-Thing opened his mouth to answer, but he was interrupted by a news flash. “This just in,” blared a voice on the store clerk’s radio. “The prison escapee with puttylike superpowers stole a car and was last seen in the desert. He is considered extremely dangerous.” The reporter stopped and chuckled. “Oh, yeah, a big fish also escaped, but he has no powers and is considered harmless.” The

store clerk heard the news and stared at Putty-Thing and Fish Guy.

"That's right, dude," Putty-Thing told the clerk. "We're criminals. Now give us your dough!"

After stealing the money, Putty-Thing decided to destroy the store. He turned his fists into hammers and smashed down the walls. Fish Guy tried to help, but he wasn't powerful at all. But Putty-Thing didn't need him. He was a one-man wrecking machine. He turned to Fish Guy and smiled. "Our work here is done, my partner in crime. It's time to jam."

They hopped into their car and raced away from the store. "We are Putty-Thing and Fish Guy," they sang happily. "We are the Terrible Two!"

"Just keep dreaming about the beach, ol' bud o' mine," Putty-Thing told Fish Guy. "'Cuz when we get to the beach, you'll be right where you belong."

Suddenly, Putty-Thing jammed on the

brakes. He stopped so fast that they tumbled up onto the hood. Fish Guy went right through Putty-Thing's puttylike body and got stuck in the middle of it. He looked out and saw what had made Putty-Thing stop.

In the middle of the road stood The Mask! "You're busted, dudes," he shouted.

Putty-Thing sneered. "Well, if it isn't that bad news green-head guy who put us in the brig in the first place!"

The Mask leaned toward the Terrible Two and sniffed. "Whoooooa!" he said, waving his hand in front of his nose. The Mask's head turned into a gas mask. "Something smells fishy around here."

"He's making fun of me," Fish Guy whined to Putty-Thing. "Do something!"

Putty-Thing jumped on top of The Mask. Slowly, he began sucking The Mask into his putty body. The Mask struggled, but it was no use. “No! No!” he shouted. “This can’t be happening! Not to me! I’m The Massssssk . . . !” In seconds he was completely absorbed into Putty-Thing.

Putty-Thing coughed. A skeleton popped out of his mouth. It was The Mask’s skeleton. Putty-Thing and Fish Guy stared down at the bones.

“Wooo . . . That was awesome,” Fish Guy said.

“I didn’t know I had such gnarly powers,” Putty-Thing agreed, pleased by his work. “Let’s get going.”

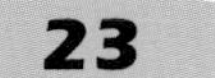

Just then, the skeleton on the ground jumped up!

"Aaaaaah!" the Terrible Two screamed.

The skeleton whirled around and around and turned into The Mask! "Psyche! Psyche!" The Mask shouted. He reached out and grabbed Putty-Thing, tossing him onto the hood of the car. He pounded him as if he were giving him a rough massage. "Been under stress lately?" he asked Putty-Thing. "Here, have some more."

Next, The Mask went after Fish Guy. The Mask's face turned into that of a sea captain. In his hand he held a huge harpoon. "I see the whale!" he called to Fish Guy. The Mask lifted his harpoon as if he were about to spear Fish Guy. Suddenly, though, The Mask stopped short as the sky filled with a deafening sound.

The sound was coming from helicopters hovering just above them. The Terrible Two stared at each other in amazement. Real helicopters had come to get them! It made them feel important. "We'll be *celebs* back in prison," Fish Guy said proudly.

The Mask looked up at the helicopters and waved. "You can take it from here!" he called to them. "I softened 'em up for ya!" A bright beam of light shot down from the helicopter. It didn't shine on Putty-Thing and Fish Guy, though. Instead, it trapped The Mask in its blindingly bright ray. The Mask couldn't move! This was no regular light beam! The Mask was caught in a laser beam! "Errrrrgggggggg!" he cried.

"Hey, let's go," Putty-Thing said, jumping back into the car. "They busted the wrong guy!"

A van pulled up next to The Mask, and its back doors swung open. The laser beams moved the helpless Mask into the back of the van. Agent X and Crosby sat in the front. "Now we can bring the alien to our underground base for laboratory experiments," Agent X said happily.

They drove to the base and put The Mask into a plain, white cell. Agent X and Crosby watched him from behind a one-way mirror. They could see The Mask, but The Mask couldn't see them. Or so they thought. "Begin the experiments," Agent X said. Crosby turned a large dial. At once, The Mask's cell began to spin, pressing The Mask to the side of the cell as if he were in a crazy carnival ride.

"Wheeee!" The Mask laughed, enjoying the spinning room.

The Mask decided to have some fun. He spun and stretched himself until he became Mime Mask. "Now I will pretend to be in a box," he said with a fake French accent. He pressed his hands against the one-way mirror, acting like someone trying to escape from inside a box.

"What is he, some kind of clown?" Agent X grumbled. "Crosby, speed it up."

The room went so fast that The Mask's face stretched back until it looked flat. Still, The Mask thought it was funny. "It's a new look . . . but I like it," he joked.

No matter what Agent X and Crosby did to The Mask, he just kept joking around. "Bombard him with gamma rays, X rays, microwaves and high-intensity radiation," Agent X ordered Crosby. Crosby turned all

the dials at once. The cell in front of them turned into a blur of dizzying waves of static. Something knocked hard against the one-way mirror.

The Mask's face appeared, cutting through the clouds of static. "Do not attempt to adjust your set," he said, talking like a TV announcer. "We control all that you see and hear."

Agent X slammed his fist against the controls. "He thinks this is a joke!" he screamed.

"His alien body may be composed of electromagnetic particles. Perhaps we should try altering his brain waves," Crosby suggested.

Agent X jumped to his feet excitedly. "Do it!" he shouted. "Break him! Break him!"

Crosby hit all the switches at once. He zapped The Mask with every kind of ray, beam, cloud, and light wave possible. The Mask clutched his head. "My brain! What are you doing to my bra-a-a-i-i-n?"

Agent X was pleased. The alien was cracking, and he'd soon reveal his plan to destroy Earth. But when he looked into the cell, he saw that The Mask had stretched himself into the shape of a hippie from the 1960s. He had a beard and long hair and wore a string of beads around his neck. "Groovy party," The Mask told Agent X.

"Where's the pulverizing switch?" Agent X screamed. "I'm gonna vaporize this clown!"

At that moment, the door burst open. Kellaway and Doyle rushed in. “Hold it!” Kellaway bellowed. “I’m taking this clown into custody!”

Agent X refused to let Kellaway take The Mask. In minutes the two men were fighting — kicking, hitting, choking, and karate-chopping one another. The Mask appeared in the room. He had changed himself into a bouncer, a person who stops fights. "Break it up," he ordered them. "Take it outside! No brawling in the secret installation."

Both men froze and stared in amazement. "How did you get out of your cell?"

The Mask shrugged. "That old thing? I just stuck around because you're almost as amusing as ol' Lieutenant Kellaway here. In fact you remind me of him." The Mask put his arm around Kellaway. "I never expected you to come rescue me. Thanks."

"I didn't come to rescue you. I came to arrest you!" Kellaway said, stamping his foot.

Now, The Mask was wearing a bowling shirt. He grinned and put his other arm around Agent X. "You knuckleheads are so much fun. How about we catch a movie or go bowling or something?"

Agent X and Kellaway couldn't stand any more of The Mask's antics. Growling with rage, they both leaped on him. At least, they *tried* to leap on him. But The Mask was too fast. He zipped out of the way, and the two men wound up leaping on each other. The Mask bounced off the walls and ceiling, then disappeared right out the door.

While all this was going on, the Terrible Two were nearing the beach. “I’m cold,” Fish Guy complained.

“We’re almost there,” Putty-Thing assured him. He saw a bunny standing on the side of the road, and his eyes narrowed meanly. “Watch me get him,” he boasted, aiming the car right for the defenseless little animal.

In a flash, The Mask was there to whisk the bunny out of the way! “Wow! That was a fast bunny!” Fish Guy gasped. The Mask was so fast that the Terrible Two hadn’t even seen him.

“Must have been some kind of super bunny,” Putty-Thing agreed.

Fish Guy began to sob loudly. “That bunny has better powers than me.” Just then, the Maskmobile pulled up alongside

them. This time, The Mask looked like a hot-rod driver. He challenged Putty-Thing to a race. “Are you chicken?” he taunted, changing his mask face into that of a chicken. This made the Terrible Two very upset.

The Mask changed back to a hot rodder. “Maybe the only driving game you guys know is *Go Fish*!” he shouted.

“He’s making fun of me again!” Fish Guy complained. Putty-Thing stepped on the gas. The race was on!

Putty-Thing slammed into the Maskmobile. The Mask just laughed and pretended to be a TV game show host. “Congratulations! You’ve just won your very own, brand-new *Fish Wizard*! It guts, scales, and fillets—everything you ever wanted to do to a fish, and more!”

Putty-Thing smashed the Maskmobile with his giant hammer fists. The Mask didn't care. He sat back and read a comic book while driving with his bare feet. Putty-Thing continued pounding the Maskmobile. He didn't notice The Mask taking a giant cartoon mallet from his book and standing up in the front seat. *Boink!* The Mask clobbered Putty-Thing flat. "Somebody stop me," The Mask cackled as he raced off down the road.

"Take the wheel," Putty-Thing told Fish Guy. He popped back into his regular shape and crawled out onto the hood. Then he used his super powers to stretch his putty arms forward. He stretched and stretched until he was able to grab the Maskmobile's fender.

"Hey!" The Mask shouted as the Maskmobile jerked to a sudden stop.

Fish Guy struggled to control the car. "I can't drive!" he shouted, terrified. Putty-Thing wasn't listening. He'd stretched himself over onto the Maskmobile, ready to fight The Mask.

Suddenly, The Mask changed into Sumo Wrestler Mask. He tried to grab hold of Putty-Thing, but Putty-Thing easily slipped away every time. "Please hold still," Sumo Wrestler Mask pleaded. He looked over at Putty-Thing and saw that half of Putty-Thing was still on the other car, which Fish Guy was driving.

"One moment, please," The Mask said politely. He ran over the top of Putty-Thing toward Fish Guy. "Hey, pal, where did you get your license? In a box of goldfish food?" he asked Fish Guy. Fish Guy was so shocked that he steered right off the road, pulling the Maskmobile and Putty-Thing with him.

Both cars sped together toward the ocean. Putty-Thing was stretched and pulled as the cars spun wildly out of control. "Hey!" Fish Guy cried out happily, noticing the beach ahead of them. "We're here!"

The Mask was confused. "We're where?"

At that moment, Putty-Thing snapped. Fish Guy screamed as his car spun across the sand. The Mask quickly clicked on a dozen seat belts and put on a crash helmet. In the next seconds, Fish Guy's car roared across the beach and out onto a long pier. Both the Maskmobile and the other car plunged into the water.

But, in the next moment, the Maskmobile bobbed up on the waves. It had turned into a space capsule. And The Mask was now an astronaut. "The eagle has landed!" he sang out.

The Terrible Two's car also floated up. So did Putty-Thing. But the water had turned him to a gooey mess. "You're a fish. You're in your element," he called to Fish Guy, who splashed helplessly nearby. "Get the green guy!"

But Fish Guy couldn't swim!

The Mask had climbed onto the end of the pier. He gazed down at Putty-Thing and Fish Guy, who were still in the water. "You're not only a lame mutant," he told Fish Guy. "You're a lame *fish*!" He turned to Putty-Thing. "And *you're* polluting the environment." He fished the Terrible Two out of the water with a net and plopped them onto the dock.

Fish Guy coughed and sputtered. Putty-Thing tried to make a hammer fist, but couldn't. He just oozed there helplessly.

“Now you’re putty in my hands,” The Mask laughed.

At the other end of the beach, a car and a van sped into the parking lot. Agent X, Crosby, and two other agents jumped out of the van. Kellaway and Doyle leaped from the squad car. Instantly, Kellaway and Agent X started fighting. “He’s a criminal!” Kellaway bellowed at Agent X.

“He’s an alien!” Agent X shot back.

“A criminal!” Kellaway insisted.

They hurried across the beach, still shouting at one another. Behind them, Crosby and Doyle followed, talking calmly. “I think he’s just misunderstood,” Doyle said.

“According to my computer analysis, he’s just some guy in a weird mask,” Crosby added.

As the men reached the pier, an eerie light filled the sky. The Spacemaskmobile hovered above them. The door of the Spacemaskmobile opened and a rope ladder dropped down. Then The Mask appeared in the doorway. He was wearing a silver space suit and a crazy-looking antenna bobbed from his headpiece. "Greetings . . . Earth creatures," he said, speaking in a high, choppy voice, as though he really *were* a space alien. "I am an intergalactic security agent, not

unlike yourselves." He reached down and picked up the Terrible Two from the pier. "My true mission was to apprehend the villainous Earth mutants and deliver them to your custody." The Spacemaskmobile floated above Agent X. The Mask dropped the criminals at his feet. "Only you could understand the cosmic threat they posed. I know you will ensure their permanent captivity." The Mask waved his hand. "Farewell, my Earth friends. And watch the skies!"

As the Spacemaskmobile zoomed away, Agent X fell to his knees. "There *is* other life in the universe," he said, tears running down his face. Then he took a deep breath and turned to Kellaway. "*Tollllld* ya he was an alien."

Kellaway still didn't believe it. "He's a common . . ." he began. But Agent X had strutted away, proud of being right. "Oh, forget it," Kellaway mumbled.

In the parking lot, the Terrible Two were loaded into Agent X's van. Kellaway and Doyle watched the van pull away. "Aliens, shmaliens," Kellaway grumbled.

As he spoke, the Spacemaskmobile zoomed right over his head. It sent down a shaft of blinding light that caught Kellaway in its beam. The light lifted Kellaway into the air. "Waahh!" he cried out in terror, as his legs kicked in the air.

Still looking like an alien, The Mask popped his head out the door. “We do exist,” he told the floating Kellaway. “And we are not so different as you think.” With a laugh and a wink, The Mask went back inside the Spacemaskmobile. Kellaway dropped the short distance to the ground as the Spacemaskmobile zoomed out of sight.

Jumping to his feet, Kellaway waved his fists in the air furiously. “I’ll get you . . . you . . . Maaaaaassssk!”